Race for the Ring

Based on the episodes "Prisoner on the Mountain" and
"Race Up Mystery Mountain"

Ready-to-Read

Simon Spotlight
New York   London   Toronto   Sydney   New Delhi

SIMON SPOTLIGHT
An imprint of Simon & Schuster Children's Publishing Division
1230 Avenue of the Americas, New York, New York 10020
This Simon Spotlight edition May 2019
Adapted by Delphine Finnegan from the series PJ Masks
SIMON SPOTLIGHT, READY-TO-READ, and colophon are registered trademarks of
Simon & Schuster, Inc.
For information about special discounts for bulk purchases, please contact
Simon & Schuster Special Sales at 1-866-506-1949 or business@simonandschuster.com
Manufactured in the United States of America 0319 LAK
10 9 8 7 6 5 4 3 2 1
ISBN 978-1-5344-4039-5 (hc)
ISBN 978-1-5344-4038-8 (pbk)
ISBN 978-1-5344-4040-1 (eBook)

Connor, Greg, and Amaya want to see a scroll at the museum.

The scroll shows the way
to Mystery Mountain.

It is missing! Amaya
knows Night Ninja has
taken it.
The PJ Masks will find it!

Connor becomes Catboy!

Amaya becomes Owlette!

Greg becomes Gekko!

They are the PJ Masks!

They look for Night Ninja.

PJ Robot helps.

Catboy hears Night Ninja.

They follow him.

Their PJ Rovers get stuck in mud.

They must stop Night Ninja before he reaches the top and gets a powerful ring!

They race toward
the mountain.

PJ Robot goes with them.

PJ Robot sees Night Ninja.

Catboy tries to
catch him!

Night Ninja throws sticky
vines to stop them.

Catboy gets stuck.

Owlette frees him but she

gets stuck too!

Night Ninja and the
Ninjalinos reach the top
of the mountain.

Catboy sees the gate that hides the magical ring!

"Out of my way,"
Night Ninja tells Catboy.

Night Ninja runs into the door and falls backward.

Catboy and Night Ninja
try to reach the gates.

The dragon statues light up, and their sticky splat tongues catch Catboy and Night Ninja!

Gekko and Owlette save Catboy and Night Ninja before the gate closes.

PJ Robot decodes
the scroll's secret
message.

Mountain splats fall from the sky. Everyone races down the mountain.

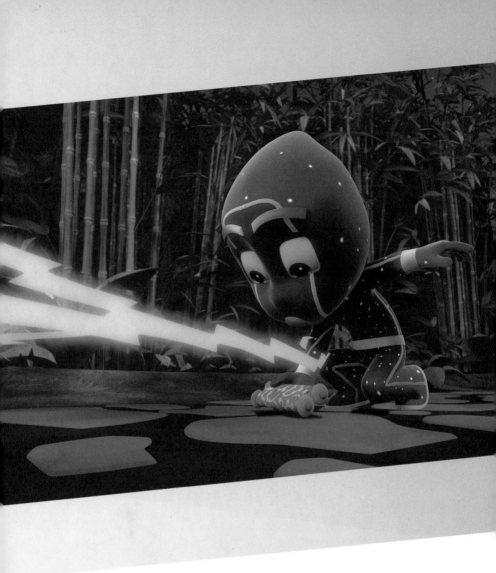

Catboy's Cat Stripes
catch Night Ninja and pull
him away from Mystery
Mountain.

Night Ninja warns,
"This isn't over,
PJ Pests!"

The PJ Masks are ready
for whatever comes next.

PJ Masks save the day!